# Forget
# This!

By Tracey West

Illustrated by the Disney Storybook Art Team

Random House 🏠 New York

# Welcome to Headquarters!

Meet the Five Emotions who live inside Riley's mind: Joy, Sadness, Anger, Disgust, and Fear. They help Riley make decisions. What should she wear today? What should she eat? Where should she sit during lunch? Riley's Emotions are with her every step of the way.

It's been two months since Joy and Sadness got sucked into the Mind World and Riley almost ran away from home. Joy and Sadness have vowed never to leave Headquarters again, because Riley needs all of her Emotions to get her through each day.

But now Anger is on a mission, and it's up to you to help him. He's going into the Mind World to stop an obnoxious jingle from playing over and over in Riley's brain. Depending on the path you choose, Anger will travel into the unknown with either Fear or Disgust. Will you help Anger succeed? Or will you get stuck in the Mind World?

Inside Headquarters, Sadness gazes longingly through the big window that looks into the Mind World. She lets out a sigh.

"Not again, Sadness," says Joy.

"I can't help it," Sadness says. "It's sad. We'll never get to go back to the Mind World again. I'll never ride on the Train of Thought. Or visit Imagination Land. All I have are my memories."

"That was an exciting adventure for sure, but you know we can't leave Headquarters," Joy reminds her. "Remember what happened to Riley the last time we were out there? She almost ran away from home! We can't risk that happening again."

Fear shudders. "I don't even know why you'd want to go back there, Sad-ness. That place is swarming with danger. Collapsing islands! A runaway train! A creepy clown! I'm glad I never got whisked out there."

"I'm glad I never got whisked out there with you," says Disgust.

"Well, I, for one, wouldn't mind giving some of those mind workers a piece of *my* mind," says Anger. "Especially those good-for-nothing Forgetters!"

Fear rolls his eyes. "Here he goes again."

"How can you NOT be upset?" Anger asks, fuming. "Those guys get to decide what Riley forgets and what she remembers. And then, just for FUN, they send annoying memories up here to bug her, like that TOTALLY WORTH-LESS Mintyblast gum jingle!"

"Aw, come on, Anger. The Forgetters are basically harmless," Joy tells him. "And anyway, that jingle *is* pretty darn catchy."

"TRAITOR!" Anger cries. "How can you take their side?"

Before Joy can answer, Disgust points to the screen that shows the Emotions the world from Riley's point of view.

"Looks like it's bedtime," she says as Riley's face appears in the bathroom mirror. "Seriously, though, Riley needs to brush her hair tonight. I refuse to let her wake up with those awful knots again in the morning."

Riley puts toothpaste on her toothbrush, then holds it up to her mouth and starts to sing:

*"Mintyblast gum makes your mouth feel clean...."*

"THAT'S IT!" Anger shouts. "There it is again! I'm going out to the Mind World to set those Forgetters straight."

Anger stomps over to the vacuum tube that carries memories in and out of Headquarters. That's how Joy and Sadness got to the Mind World.

"Whoa there, bucko!" Joy says as she jumps in front of him. "Let's all just take a breather here."

Anger growls.

"All right, not a fan of breathing, I get it," Joy quickly replies. "But you can't leave! Riley needs you. What if Matt Fletcher tries to steal the basketball from her in gym class again?"

"Riley is about to go to sleep," Anger says through gritted teeth. "I'll go now and come right back."

Joy considers this. "Well . . ."

"If you go, you'll probably never come back, and we'll never see you again," Sadness whimpers.

"Don't go," Fear pleads. "You'll get trapped in the Subconscious with an evil clown!"

*"Mintyblast gum is so extreme!"* Riley sings.

"I'll take the chance," Anger says. "If I hear that jingle one more time, I'll . . . I'm gonna—"

"What?" asks Disgust. "You'll finish your sentence?"

"Okay, you can go," Joy interjects before Anger explodes. "Riley will be a lot happier if she gets that jingle out of her brain.

"When the chute spits you out, just head toward the rows of shelves," explains Joy. "That's Long Term Memory."

"And stay away from the cliffs," Fear adds.

"Yeah, yeah. Shelves, good. Cliffs, bad. I get it," Anger says.

Riley finishes brushing her teeth. She goes to her room, yawns, and climbs into bed. In just a few minutes, she's asleep, and she starts dreaming right away.

"All right, I'm out of here!" Anger announces.

"Wait!" Disgust says. "I think she's having that dream again."

Riley's dream plays on the big screen. In it, Riley sees herself sleeping in bed. But then she wakes up—and her hair has turned into streams of creepy-crawly spiders!

"Aaaaaah!" screams Fear.

"Gross!" Disgust shrieks. "Why does she keep having this dream? Are the Forgetters doing this, too?"

"No, the dreams are made in Dream Productions," Joy explains. "I'm not sure who creates them. A dream director, maybe."

"Well, this director must be pretty demented to keep turning Riley's hair into spiders every night," Disgust says. Then she turns to Anger. "I'm going with you. I've got to stop this dream."

"What? No way," Anger insists. "This is a one-man operation."

"If you both go, you'll both be lost forever," Sadness says with a sigh. "We'll miss you."

"Nobody is getting lost forever!" Anger shouts. "I am going *by myself* to persuade the Forgetters to see things my way." He smacks his fist into his hand to make his point. "Then I'm coming right back here."

"And I am going with you, to tell the dream director to cool it with the spiders," Disgust says firmly.

Up on the screen, in her dream, Riley is shampooing her hair, trying to get the spiders out. But the bathtub just keeps filling with spiders.

"Riley doesn't sleep well when she has dreams like this, and that affects her whole day," Joy reasons. "Anger, maybe you should let Disgust go with you."

If Anger and Disgust go to the Mind World together, go to page 67.

If Anger goes to the Mind World by himself, go to page 96.

(continued from page 119)

Anger hates to admit it, but he sees Disgust's point. He's not getting anywhere with these annoying Forgetters.

"Fine," he whispers. "You try. But if you mess up, I'm jumping back in!"

"Just watch," Disgust says.

Smiling, she steps between Anger and the Forgetters and bats her long eyelashes.

"Don't mind my little red friend here," she says. "I'm sure you guys know what you're doing."

"Of course we do," says one Forgetter. "We keep things in order down here. And if we send back a fun little memory once in a while, what's the harm?"

"I like that jingle," says the other Forgetter. "It's catchy. *Mintyblast gum is so extreme!*"

Behind Disgust, Anger starts to fume. She can practically feel the heat radiating from him.

"Yeah, that's a great jingle," Disgust agrees. "It's just, you know, even the best jingles get a little old, right? Like, Mintyblast is just so yesterday."

The Forgetters look at each other.

"Are we old?" asks one.

"And out of touch?" asks the other.

Disgust shrugs. "I'm not saying that. It's just that, you know, Mintyblast doesn't have even a thousand followers on Tweeter."

The Forgetters frown. "Hey, are you trying to

use some kind of psychology on us?" says the first one.

"I'm just trying to have a conversation," Disgust replies.

The Forgetters whisper to each other. Then they turn back to Disgust.

"We'll get rid of the jingle," says the first Forgetter. "*If* you do something for us."

"Like what?" Disgust asks.

"We want French fries from Imagination Land," he replies.

Anger can't keep his mouth shut anymore. "*French fries*? What for?"

"Riley has lots of French fry memories, but we've never seen one up close," the other Forgetter explains. "We never get any time off. This is a full-time job."

"And Riley loves the smell of fries so much that we're curious about them," says the other. "We're curious beings."

"More like weird beings," Anger mutters.

"We'll do it!" says Disgust. "See you guys in a flash."

She drags Anger away before he can say anything else.

"This shouldn't be too hard," she says. "I mean, French fries are fast food, right?"

The two Emotions emerge from the shelves of Long Term Memory and look out across the plateau. In the distance, they see a colorful wall with gates on the left and the right.

"That must be it over there," Disgust says. "Which gate should we go through?"

If they enter through the left gate, go to page 72.

If they enter through the right gate, go to page 111.

"Let's just take the purple one and toss it into the Memory Dump!" Anger says.

"But what if it's the wrong memory?" Disgust asks.

"It's not wrong," Anger insists. "You can see the memory playing inside. Look!"

Disgust peers into the sphere. "Gross!" she shrieks.

"Told you!" Anger says. He grabs the purple sphere and marches off toward the cliffs that overlook the Memory Dump. Rainbow Unicorn and Disgust follow him.

Anger reaches the edge of the cliff and looks down. All the memories that Riley no longer needs are sent to the Dump. They stay there until they dissolve into mist.

"So long, spiders!" Anger says. He hurls the purple sphere over the cliff. Then he walks back to Disgust and Rainbow Unicorn. "Good riddance! No spiders, no dream. Now let's go

find those Forgetters."

Rainbow Unicorn blocks his path. "Excuse me. You were going to help me come up with a fabulous new dream, remember?"

"Yeah, yeah, but we don't have time for that right now, lady," Anger says. "Step aside."

Rainbow Unicorn doesn't budge. Her nostrils flare, and her eyes flash. "Do you really want to mess with me, little man?"

Anger clears his throat. "Well, when you put it that way . . ."

Moments later they're back at Dream Productions. The director races up to them.

"You guys did it!" she says. "It was like, *poof!*

and suddenly our writing staff couldn't come up with another word about spiders. We've got to get a new dream going, stat. You have something for me, Rainbow?"

"We're working it up right now," Rainbow Unicorn says. "Let's go, crew."

"Crew?" says Disgust. "You've got it wrong. I'm your costar. I've got the whole thing figured out. . . ."

"Stop right there!"

Two mind workers run up on their tiny legs. Anger recognizes them from Joy and Sadness's description.

"Forgetters!" he yells.

"Robbers!" yells one of the Forgetters. "You stole a memory from the shelves. Nobody can do that but us!"

"Says who?" asks Anger.

"Says us," says his partner. "And now we're sending *you* to the Subconscious."

"Ugh! No way," says Disgust.

"Way!" says the first Forgetter.

Disgust and Anger look at each other.

"Run!" they yell.

They speed out of Dream Productions, not really sure where they're headed. Riley's Islands of Personality are in front of them.

Disgust looks behind her. "They're gaining on us!"

"That looks like Hockey Island over there," says Anger.

"And that's Honesty Island," says Disgust. "Which way should we go?"

If they flee to Honesty Island, go to page 106.

If they head to Hockey Island, go to page 120.

(continued from page 99)

"Buildings have walls. Walls are safe," says Fear as he runs toward the buildings.

"Where are you going?" Anger yells, chasing after him. But Anger's stubby legs are no match for Fear's long ones and his nervous energy.

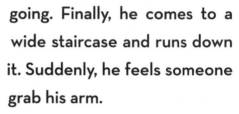

Fear keeps running, not sure where he's going. Finally, he comes to a wide staircase and runs down it. Suddenly, he feels someone grab his arm.

"Troublemaker, eh?" says a guard. "Come with me."

Anger appears at the top of the stairs, huffing and puffing.

"LET MY FRIEND GO!" he yells, running down the stairs to help Fear.

"Another troublemaker!" says the guard.

A second guard grabs Anger. "Stop right there, troublemaker!"

"Get your hands off me!" Anger yells.

But the guard grips him tightly. The two guards push Anger and Fear toward a creepy-looking building.

"What is this place?" Fear asks nervously.

"Weren't you listening to Joy and Sadness?" Anger asks. "This is Riley's Subconscious!"

Fear remembers the stories. "Noooooooo!" he cries.

The guards open a door, push Fear and Anger inside, and shut the door behind them. Inside, it's pitch-black.

"Can somebody please turn on the lights?" Fear calls out.

*Cluck, cluck, cluck!*

Fear jumps. "What was that?"

"It sounds like chickens," says Anger.

"Regular chickens or monster chickens?" Fear asks.

"There's no such thing as monster chickens," Anger says.

"How can you be sure?" Fear asks.

"Chickens are the least of our worries," says Anger. "When Joy and Sadness were here, they ran into Jangles the birthday clown, remember? He was sleeping, but he woke up. So be very quiet, okay?"

"Okay," says Fear. Then something flies by. "MONSTER CHICKEN!" he yells.

"Oh, brother," says Anger.

*Honk! Honk!* The sound of a bicycle horn fills the air. Then the lights flicker on. A huge clown with a creepy smile towers over them.

"Who's the birthday girl?" Jangles asks.

Fear freezes.

Anger wants to run, but he can't leave Fear behind.

If Anger stands up to Jangles, go to page 37.

If Anger tries to unfreeze Fear, go to page 75.

"We're done talking," says one of the Forgetters. "Are you going to do us another favor or not?"

Anger looks like he's about to blow up again, but Disgust stops him.

"Just tell us what you want," she says. "But say please this time."

"Fine," says the other Forgetter. "*Please* bring us a hockey stick and a hockey puck from Hockey Island."

"What do you need those for?" Disgust asks.

Now it's Anger's turn to interrupt. "At least hockey is something I understand. Let's just go and get this over with."

"And make it snappy!" one Forgetter calls out as Disgust and Anger walk away.

The two Emotions head over to Hockey Island.

"Wow, it's really beautiful here," says Disgust,

gazing at the islands as they get closer.

"That's Riley for you. She has a beautiful mind," says Anger.

As they approach Hockey Island, they feel a chill in the air. A huge ice-skating arena sits in the middle of the island.

"Boy, do I love hockey!" says Anger. "When Riley slams that puck . . . whoa! It feels great!"

"Yeah, well, I hate how sweaty she gets when she plays," says Disgust. "How can she get so sweaty when she's on the ice? It doesn't make any sense."

When they set foot on the island, they find an equipment shed outside the arena. It's loaded with hockey sticks and pucks. They grab one of each for the Forgetters and make the journey back to Long Term Memory.

"Yippee!" says the girl Forgetter when she sees the stick and puck. "Now we can have some fun!"

"Wait? How can *we* have some fun?" asks the other Forgetter. "There's only one stick and one puck."

"Hold it right there!" says Anger. "One stick. One puck. That was the deal. NOW GET RID OF THAT JINGLE!"

The Forgetters don't argue. They quickly recall the memory sphere from the shelves of Long Term Memory and vacuum it up into the Memory Dump.

"All done," says the girl Forgetter.

"Thank you," says Disgust. She turns to Anger. "Now we can go to Dream Productions."

"No you can't, because they're about to close," the boy Forgetter reports.

Disgust scowls.

"Well, at least we got rid of that jingle!" says Anger.

# THE END

Disgust nudges Anger.

"Apologize," she hisses.

Anger really, really hates to do it. But he swallows his pride.

"Fine," he says. "I'm sorry for calling you jerks."

"We don't accept your apology," one For-getter says.

"And we won't help you," says the other. "You're a big meanie!"

"Then why did you make me apologize?" yells Anger.

Disgust grabs his arm. "Forget about it. These guys won't help us. Let's go to Dream Productions before you make things worse."

"Let's race again," says Anger.

Disgust sighs. "Okay. The first one to the end of that row of shelves wins. Ready . . . go!"

They begin to run as fast as they can.

Go to page 44.

(continued from page 125)

"That's a kitten costume!" says Anger. He holds it up. The suit is made of soft gray fur. There's a long white tail with a soft white puffball on the end. The ears are pink inside.

"NO WAY!" he yells, startling Fear.

Fear knocks over a barrel of tennis rackets, which spill out onto the stage. In the dream, they look like beavers with flat tails. The beavers start juggling the eyeballs.

"This has gone far enough," growls the director. "Stagehands! Get them out of here!"

Six small but strong stagehands grab Anger and Fear. They walk them out of Dream Productions.

"Hey! Easy!" says Anger.

Fear finally starts to calm down. "Are we going home now?" he asks.

The stagehands don't answer. They march Anger

and Fear to Long Term Memory, find a recall tube, and shove the two Emotions inside.

"You're back!" Joy cries, hugging them as they spill into Headquarters.

"Did you get rid of the jingle?" Sadness asks.

"No," snaps Anger. "And I don't want to talk about it!" He stomps off.

Disgust is staring at the spider, snakes, and eyeball-juggling beavers on the screen. "Is anyone else seeing this?" she asks. "This is the worst dream ever! Tomorrow night, I'm going down there by myself if I have to!"

## THE END

(continued from page 102)

"I'M LEAVING!" Anger yells over the music. "ARE YOU COMING WITH ME?"

Disgust ignores him, cheering for the boys on the screen.

"FORGET IT! I'M OUT OF HERE!" Anger yells again. He marches all the way back to Long Term Memory.

"Where are our French fries?" the Forgetters ask when he arrives.

"The deal is off!" Anger replies. "No French fries for you! Just get me out of this crazy place!"

The Forgetters lead Anger to a recall tube. Anger crawls inside the tube. Then . . . *whoosh!* He tumbles into Headquarters.

"You're back!" Fear cries. "But where's Disgust?"

"Going gaga over some pop stars on Boy Band Island," Anger says. "I had to leave her behind."

Sadness sighs. "I knew it. We'll never see her again."

"We'll see her, because you're going back to find her," Joy tells Sadness. "You'll have to do it tomorrow night, because Riley is going to wake up soon."

Fear puts his hands to his mouth. "Riley will have to spend a day without Disgust? I bet all kinds of bad things will happen. I'm not sure what they are, I just bet that they will."

Riley wakes up a short while later. She starts humming the Mintyblast jingle.

"Oh, dear. You mean you went through all that and didn't get rid of the jingle?" Sadness asks Anger.

"Let's just say that things didn't go as planned," Anger says.

Then Fear notices something. "Hey, did Riley brush her teeth?"

"Um, I don't know," admits Joy.

Riley puts a piece of bread in the toaster. The Emotions see her reflection.

"Oh, dear. Look at that big knot in her hair," Sadness says. "That's never going to come out."

The Emotions watch the screen all morning. How will Riley get through the day at school with bad breath and bad hair? Around noon, Disgust tumbles out of the recall tube.

"Finally!" Anger yells.

Disgust brushes off her dress. "Sorry. I was having a good time on Boy Band Island, but those guys just kept singing the same five songs over and over again. I got bored," she says. "Is Riley awake?"

The Emotions nod to the screen. Riley is in the bathroom at school, looking at herself in the mirror. Her hair is a mess. Disgust screams.

"You should have come with me," Anger says.

## THE END

(continued from page 26)

Anger pushes aside the feeling of terror rising up inside him. It's time to do what he does best.

"Hey, Big Nose!" he yells. "You want a birthday party? I'll show you a birthday party. Follow me!"

*Honk! Honk!* Jangles stumbles after him.

Anger picks up Fear, who's frozen like a Popsicle. Then he slowly walks backward, toward the door. He knows the guards are out there, but right now, he would rather deal with them than with this creepy clown.

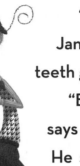

"Who's the birthday girl?" Jangles asks again, his yellow teeth gleaming in the dim light.

"Birthday party's out there," says Anger, pointing at the door. He steps aside so that Jangles can see it.

Jangles honks his horn. "It's party time!"

Then he crashes through the door. Anger hears the guards scream outside.

"We're busting out of here, buddy!" he tells Fear. Still holding Fear, he runs outside. Jangles is chasing the terrified guards around the building.

"Enjoy the party!" Anger yells at the guards. Then he makes his way back to Long Term Memory, carrying Fear the whole way.

"For a bean pole, you sure weigh a lot," he mutters.

When he reaches Long Term Memory, two

blue creatures approach him. Anger realizes they're exactly who he's been looking for—the Forgetters.

"What happened to him?" one Forgetter asks, nodding to Fear.

"He saw Jangles the clown," Anger says. "We both did. But I got us out of there."

The Forgetters' eyes grow wide. "Jangles?" they ask.

"Yeah," says Anger, suddenly getting an idea. "I took care of him. And I'll take care of you, too, unless you do me a favor."

Anger explains that he wants the gum jingle gone forever. The frightened Forgetters agree to get rid of it. Then they lead Anger to a recall tube.

"Just stuff your friend in first," says one of the Forgetters. "Then climb in after him."

"Thanks," says Anger as he shoves Fear into the tube.

*Whoosh!*

"I hope he'll be okay once he gets back to Headquarters," Anger says, then climbs in after him.

# THE END

"Give me a push. I think I can get that fork," Disgust tells Anger.

Anger obeys. Disgust reaches out with her short green arms and grabs the end of the plastic fork. She frees herself from the ketchup. Then she holds the fork out to Anger so he can get out, too.

Disgust looks down at herself. There's ketchup up to her knees.

"Well, these shoes are ruined, but my dress is fine," she says. "Now let's chop down some French fries and get out of here."

"My pleasure," says Anger.

Anger and Disgust use the plastic fork like a chain saw. They each grab an end and move the edge of the handle back and forth across a fry. It topples over like a tree.

"Let's get one more so they'll each have one," Anger suggests.

They chop down another fry. Then they

each carry one out of Imagination Land and back to Long Term Memory.

The Forgetters are eagerly waiting for them.

"French fries!" they cry.

Anger and Disgust hand over the fries.

"So that's what they look like up close," says one.

"They smell greasy and salty," says the other.

"Yup, and they're all yours," says Anger. "Now it's time to keep up your end of the bargain."

"Right." The boy Forgetter nods. He walks over to a shelf, pushes aside a panel, and presses a button. Seconds later, a glowing ball comes down the memory chute.

"One gum jingle," he says, handing the sphere to Anger.

"Let me do the honors," Anger says. He grabs the Forgetter's vacuum and sucks up the memory. "Good riddance!" he cries.

"Great," says Disgust. "Now let's go to Dream Productions and get rid of that spider dream."

"Dream Productions is closing in a few minutes," says the girl Forgetter. "It's almost morning."

"Sorry, we're out of time," Anger says.

Disgust frowns. "This is so not fair," she protests.

The Forgetters lead Disgust and Anger to a recall tube and they get sucked up to Headquarters.

"I'll be back!" Disgust promises.

## THE END

(continued from pages 31 and 70)

"I win!" Disgust cheers.

"Of course you do," says Anger, catching his breath. He stomps toward Dream Productions. "It's going to take forever to get there, you know. The Train of Thought doesn't run when Riley is asleep."

Disgust catches up with him. "It will be worth it," she says. "And once we get there, it shouldn't take long. I'll use my charm, and you can use your . . . you know . . . that intimidating thing you do, to convince the director to stop the spider dream."

Anger punches his fist into his hand again. "Yeah, I'm itching to do some convincing!"

They walk a long way to get to Dream Productions. The set is bustling with actors in costumes scurrying back and forth and a stage manager screaming directions at everyone. Onstage, actors are wearing silly-looking spider costumes with eight legs—but in Riley's dream, they look just like real spiders.

Anger stops one of the spiders. "Where's the director?" he asks.

But before he can get an answer, Disgust lets out a squeal behind him.

"Rainbow Unicorn!" she cries. She rushes over to a beautiful unicorn with a rainbow-streaked mane and a glittering horn.

"I am totally your biggest fan," Disgust says. "How do you get your hair so shiny?"

"You wouldn't believe how long it takes to condition," Rainbow Unicorn says. "Not that it matters anyway. I'm not getting screen time these days." She nods to the spiders.

"I know, right? Those spiders are awful," says Disgust. "We're here to convince the director to stop those spider dreams once and for all."

Rainbow Unicorn looks interested. "Really?

'Cause I was thinking the same thing. I could produce a super-fabulous dream starring myself and then the director will have to use it in place of those ridiculous spiders."

Disgust thinks quickly. "I know! You help us convince the director, and we'll help you produce your amazing dream!"

Rainbow Unicorn nods. "She's right over there."

Disgust and Rainbow Unicorn head over to talk to the dream director.

"Hey, where are you going?" Anger asks.

"Just come with us, and stay quiet," says Disgust. "We've got a plan."

"Oh, how nice. You and this candy-colored horse have a plan. Well, thanks for telling me!" Anger fumes.

Disgust ignores him, and marches up to the director.

"Excuse me, Director, but we have a proposal for you," she says.

The director puts her clipboard down on her lap and yawns. "Oh yeah?"

"Yeah, and it's a great one," Disgust replies. "My friend and I here are going to produce a fantastic dream starring Rainbow Unicorn."

"We are?" Anger asks.

"We are," says Disgust firmly. "And then you can stop running that spider dream. Deal?"

"I'd love to," the director says. "We're all getting tired of the spider dreams. The actors aren't wiggling like they used to. But Riley's dream is coming from a memory. She was learning about spiders in school, and it brought up a bad spider memory from a few years ago. I can't get rid of the dream while that memory's still around."

"But couldn't a fabulous dream starring Rainbow Unicorn push out some crummy old memory?" asks Rainbow Unicorn.

The director thinks. "That might work. But the dream would have to be *really* fabulous." She yells into a megaphone. "Okay, spiders, put some heart into that wiggling!"

Back in Headquarters, the spiders break into a spooky dance on the screen.

"Make it stop!" yells Fear.

If Disgust and Anger help Rainbow Unicorn produce a new dream, go to page 62.

If Disgust and Anger search for the spider memory, go to page 88.

(continued from page 110)

Anger carries Fear. In the distance, he can see Friendship Island happily humming. That's the Island of Personality that helps Riley make friends and keep her friendships strong.

Friendship Island is a happy place. Fear smiles as Anger sets him down on the ground.

"I feel so warm and fuzzy," he says.

"Great," says Anger. "Now let's you and me—"

Fear wanders off toward a gallery of photos of Riley's friends.

"Look, there's Riley's friend Katie." He points to a photo of a girl with short, brown hair. "Remember when Riley and Katie first met, and Riley went over to her house? Katie doesn't like hockey, and we were worried we couldn't be friends. But we got along great anyway. That's when Riley learned that she could be friends with somebody she didn't have a lot in common with."

Fear turns to Anger. "That's just like us," he says, giving Anger a hug. "Thanks for saving me back there, buddy."

Anger squirms uncomfortably. "Can we please go find the Forgetters now?"

Fear beams. "Sure! Anything for you, friend!"

**Go to page 114.**

A creepy sound comes out of the tunnel.

"Whatever's in there has got to be worse than broccoli," says Anger.

"NOTHING is worse than broccoli!" yells Disgust, running into the tunnel.

Anger sighs and dashes in after her.

The tunnel is filled with crazy, swirling lights. Weird shrieks and screams fill the air.

Then they hear a new sound.

"Grandma's vacuum!" Anger says. It was one of the first things ever to scare Riley when she was just a little baby. "Run!"

They race back toward the entrance. The vacuum shoots after them as if it's alive. They dive out of the way as the vacuum crashes through the broccoli and into the door!

Disgust and Anger race past the startled guards, who are also running from the vacuum.

"Let's get back to Headquarters," Disgust says. "This place is too weird!"

# THE END

**(continued from page 113)**

"There's nothing to talk about," says one of the Forgetters. "If you don't do what we want, we won't help you."

Disgust and Anger look at each other. They're both thinking the same thing.

"Forget it," says Anger. "We did what you wanted, and you broke your promise. We're not doing anything else."

"I bet I know why you two don't get to go anywhere," Disgust adds. "It's because you're rude little jerks! Nobody wants to hang out with you!"

"Yeah, you little blue creeps!" Anger says.

The Forgetters' eyes narrow. One points the vacuum at them.

"Quick! Find a recall tube!" Anger yells.

The Emotions dash off toward a nearby recall tube and jump inside. They get sucked back to Headquarters before the Forgetters can catch up to them.

"You're back!" Fear says, hugging them.

"But you didn't get rid of the spider dream," Sadness says, looking up at the screen.

"No," says Anger. "And we didn't get rid of the Mintyblast jingle, either. It's a jungle out there, I tell you."

Sadness sighs. "So you two risked it all for nothing."

"But I'm sure they had a fun adventure, just like we did," Joy says. "And they're back before Riley's awake. So it's all good."

Suddenly, they hear a *whoosh!* A recalled memory sphere shoots up through the tube.

"What is it?" Fear asks.

Joy picks up the memory sphere. "Looks like another jingle. Pitter-Patter Cat Food."

"Oh no," groans Anger.

*Whoosh! Whoosh! Whoosh!* More memory spheres shoot into Headquarters.

"They're all jingles!" Joy reports. "Munchies cereal. Lemon Fizz soda pop. Bluebird Airlines."

Anger shakes his fist. "Curse you, Forgetters!"

"I guess we shouldn't have made them angry," says Disgust.

## THE END

*(continued from page 80)*

"There's a creepy tunnel down there," Disgust says, squinting in the darkness. "Maybe it's a way out."

A scream comes from the tunnel.

"I'm not taking any chances," says Anger. "I'll push it myself!"

His red face turns even redder as he pushes the broccoli stalk. Sweat streams down his forehead. But the broccoli doesn't budge.

Another scream comes from the tunnel, followed by the sound of loud footsteps.

"Come on," Anger says. "I hate to say it, but I can't do this by myself."

"No way," Disgust protests.

Then an evil cackle comes through the tunnel. Disgust starts to panic.

"All right," she says. "I'll just close my eyes and pretend it's a big tree."

She closes her eyes and gives the broccoli stalk a push.

"Harder!" Anger yells.

Another roar comes from the tunnel.

"I'm trying!" Disgust shouts back.

They both give the broccoli a mighty shove—revealing the door behind it.

"Let's get out of here!" Anger says.

"But those guards are out there," Disgust says.

Anger eyes a piece of the giant broccoli stalk that has fallen off.

"Leave it to me," he says, picking up the broken piece of broccoli. "Okay, open the door and follow me."

"Aaaaaaaaaaaaaah!" With a mighty war cry, Anger uses the broccoli stalk like a battering ram, knocking down the two startled guards. He and Disgust don't stop running until they reach Long Term Memory. They climb inside a recall tube, just like Joy and Sadness told them to do.

*Whoosh!* They're quickly whisked to Headquarters.

"You're back!" Fear cries, hugging them.

"But Riley's still having the spider dream," Sadness says.

"Nice to see you, too," says Anger.

"Riley's still having the spider dream because the Mind World is crazy!" says Disgust. "I'm never going back there."

"You mean you didn't have an awesome adventure?" Joy asks.

"There was broccoli involved," Anger explains.

The Emotions gasp.

"I don't want to talk about it," Disgust says. "I'll take those spiders over broccoli any day!"

## THE END

"This is a kitten costume," says Anger.

"Yes, I know that," says the director dryly. "Your friend is out of control. Calm him down before Riley's dream gets crazy and she wakes up."

Anger looks at the screen and sees the spiders, snakes, and bouncing apples. He knows Riley won't like that.

He sighs. "For Riley."

Anger slips on the kitten costume. He looks ridiculous. His red face sticks out from under fluffy gray ears with pink centers. Whiskers poke out from his cheeks, and there's a fluffy white tail in the back.

With another sigh, he slowly enters the dream and approaches Fear.

"Hey there, look at me," he says. "I'm a cute little kitten."

Fear is about to knock over a barrel of tennis rackets, but he stops when he hears Anger.

The panic fades from Fear's eyes.

"I like kittens," Fear says. "Kittens are safe."

"That's right," says Anger. "Come to the safe little kitty."

Fear walks away from the stage.

"Thanks," the director says to Anger. "Now get him out of here."

"Sure," says Anger. "But maybe you can help us, too. Think you can get rid of that spider dream?"

The director nods. "It's complicated, because it's being caused by a spider memory of Riley's. But I'll get a production assistant on it right away."

"Riley!" Fear says, panicking. "We've got to get back before she wakes up."

"The jingle!" Anger protests, but Fear is already running off again.

He sees a recall tube and climbs in.

"Riley, here I come!" he says, and shoots up through the tube.

Anger follows Fear back to Headquarters.

"You're back!" Joy cries happily, hugging them.

"What was up with that weird dream with the snakes and eyeballs?" Disgust asks with a shudder.

"Long story. But it's gone, and the spider dream will be gone soon, too," Anger replies. "We're still stuck with the jingle, though."

Sadness frowns. "So you failed. That's too bad."

## THE END

"I'm not asking for favors, I'm making a demand," Anger tells Disgust, his voice rising. Then he turns back to the Forgetters.

"Listen up, you little blue jerks," Anger says. "I am not asking, I'm demanding. Get rid of that Mintyblast jingle now!"

"Who are you calling jerks, beef-a-rooney?" one Forgetter asks.

"Yeah, who?" says her partner.

"YOU!" yells Anger. Disgust rolls her eyes. This isn't going well.

"We're not doing anything for you unless you apologize," says the first Forgetter.

The other Forgetter nods. "That's right. We want a really BIG apology."

Anger scowls. Apologizing is not his style.

If Anger apologizes, go to page 31.

If he doesn't apologize, go to page 104.

61

"Well, I'm not going anywhere near that spider memory," says Disgust. "Come on. I know we can make a fabulous dream."

"You should be our director," says Rainbow Unicorn, batting her long eyelashes. "It takes a strong personality to handle a superstar like me."

"Fine. Let's get this over with," says Anger.

Disgust disappears into the costume room and returns a few minutes later. She's wearing star-shaped sunglasses, a sequined dress, a feathered headdress, and white boots. A pair of green and gold wings are strapped to her back.

"What are you supposed to be?" Anger asks.

"Stylish," Disgust replies.

A cameraman comes over, and Anger looks through the lens and sees what Riley will see in her dream—a feathered horse with huge wings and stars for eyes.

"Yeah. A stylish horse," Anger says.

"A horse? I look like a horse?" Disgust asks.

"A Pegasus," says Rainbow Unicorn.

Disgust considers this. "How about my character is Star Pegasus," she says. "And in the dream, Rainbow Unicorn is missing, and Star Pegasus has to search the world for her."

Rainbow Unicorn clears her throat. "Excuse me, but how can I be the star when I'm missing?"

"Well, I'll find you eventually," says Disgust. Then she looks down at her costume. "And anyway, we promised fabulous, and let's face it, Star Pegasus is super fabulous."

"Riley already thinks *I'm* fabulous," says Rainbow Unicorn, moving between Disgust and the camera.

Disgust shoves her aside. "But Riley hasn't seen me yet!"

Anger looks through the camera lens. The two magical creatures start leaping over each other. As they jump, sequins fly off Disgust's dress. They look like shooting stars.

The director comes over. "What's this?" she asks, looking through the lens. "Wow, amazing! Spiders, take five!"

In Headquarters, Joy, Fear, and Sadness watch the new dream playing on-screen.

"Look! No more spiders," says Joy.

"But it's almost morning," says Sadness. "Soon Riley will wake up, and Fear and Disgust won't be here. Poor Riley."

Back in Dream Productions, Disgust realizes they need to get back to Riley. "Sorry, we've got to head back to Headquarters."

"But what about the Forgetters?" Anger asks.

"No time," says Disgust. "Let's go!"

Anger and Disgust race to Long Term Memory as quickly as they can. They find a recall tube and get sucked back up to Headquarters.

"You're all right!" says Fear, running to hug them.

"Yes, yes, we're fine, except we didn't get rid of that annoying jingle," Anger says.

"But you got rid of the dream, and Riley will be happy," says Joy.

"She'll be even happier when I go back there tomorrow night, ALONE," Anger says. "I won't rest until that jingle is gone forever!"

## THE END

Anger and Fear take aim at the flower.

*Ding!* Anger looks up. A light is flashing over Fear's flower.

"I win!" cheers Fear. "I'm staying here."

"Well, I'm leaving," says Anger, stomping off. But suddenly, he stops.

What will the other Emotions say if he returns without Fear? He looks back at Fear, who's happily clutching the stuffed teddy bear he won.

With a sigh, Anger walks back to him.

"I'll stick around," he says.

Fear hugs him. "Thanks, pal."

Anger cringes. He hopes Fear will get sick of this place soon so they can get back to Head-quarters!

# THE END

Anger lets out an exasperated sigh.

"Fine," he says. "But if you mess things up for me, I'm stuffing your green self right back into that memory chute."

"I'm not the one who messes things up around here," says Disgust. She turns to Joy. "Okay, how do we do this, again?"

"Last time, Sadness and I got sucked into the memory chute accidentally," Joy explains.

"But you guys should be able to jump right in."

Anger stuffs himself into the chute. "I'm coming for you, Forgetters!" he yells.

Disgust jumps in after him.

*Whoosh!* The chute sucks them through the long tube that leads all the way across the Mind World to Long Term Memory.

Inside Headquarters, Sadness shakes her head. "It won't be the same around here without them."

"Sadness and I came back. They will, too," Joy promises. She looks up at the screen. "I just hope they're back before Riley wakes up. She needs all her Emotions when she's awake!"

A few moments later, Anger and Disgust tumble out into the Mind World.

They stand up and look around. They're on a wide plateau, and in the distance they can see the long stacks of shelves that hold

Riley's memories. There are some other buildings beyond them.

Anger marches toward the shelves. "I'm going to find those Forgetters."

Disgust follows him. "Oh no," she says. "We are going to Dream Productions first."

"Let's do rock-paper-scissors," Anger suggests.

Disgust nods. "All right. One, two, three!"

Anger throws out a clenched fist, and Disgust holds out a flat hand.

"Ha!" she says. "I win!"

"Paper doesn't beat rock," Anger says. "Rock smashes paper. Smashes it!"

Now Disgust frowns. "We're never going to

get back before Riley wakes up. Let's try something else. How about a race?"

"A race? That's ridiculous."

Disgust puts her hands on her hips. "What's the matter? Afraid you can't beat me?"

"Of course not," says Anger.

"Then let's race to the edge of that cliff over there," Disgust says, pointing. "If I win, we go to Dream Productions. If you win, we go to Long Term Memory."

"Fine," says Anger.

If Disgust wins the race, go to page 44.

If Anger wins, go to page 116.

70

(continued from page 83)

Anger and Fear aim their water pistols at the flowers.

*Ding!* Anger looks up. A light is flashing above his flower.

"I win!" he says. "You're coming back with me!"

"Do I have to?" Fear asks.

"I won fair and square," Anger tells him.

Fear nods. "All right," he says with a sigh.

Anger hands him the teddy bear he just won. "Here, this is for you."

Fear beams. "Thanks!"

Clutching the teddy bear, Fear makes it back to Long Term Memory without freaking out. Anger doesn't even bother to look for the Forgetters. Putting up with the Mintyblast jingle is a lot easier than traveling around the Mind World with Fear!

# THE END

"The left one's closer," says Anger. "Let's get this over with."

They quickly head toward Imagination Land. Beyond the gates they glimpse crazy colors and things moving, but it's difficult to tell what's going on inside.

They enter through the left gate and see a sign for Trophy Town. Past the sign are tall, shining trophies that Riley has imagined she'll win one day.

"'Women's Ice Hockey Champion of the Universe,'" Anger reads. "If anyone can do that, it's Riley!"

Disgust is more interested in the shiny surface of the trophies. She stops in front of a silver one and gazes at her reflection.

"Just look at my hair," she wails. "It's terrible!"

"It looks exactly the same as it always does," Anger points out.

"It does?" Disgust asks, checking her reflection again. She strikes a pose with her hands on her hips. "Hmm. Maybe it's not so bad. And you know, I kind of like the glow of the trophies around here. It complements my complexion."

Anger rolls his eyes. "Hello? We're supposed to find French Fry Forest, remember?"

Disgust ignores him and runs over to a gold trophy with a wide cup. It distorts her reflection and makes her eyes look huge.

"Wow, this is awesome," Disgust says. "Look how long my lashes are!"

"Yes," Anger says, rolling his eyes again. "Now can we go?"

But Disgust won't break away from her reflection.

"Fine, stay here," Anger fumes. "I'll find those stupid French fries all by myself."

He starts to stomp off, then stops. Joy warned them to stick together. Is it a good idea to leave Disgust behind?

If Anger storms off, go to page 86.

If he tries to find a way to get Disgust out of there, go to page 100.

Jangles honks his horn again and starts dancing, hopping from one foot to the other. His big, red shoes flop up and down like giant tongues.

"Happy birthday!" he yells.

Anger turns and faces Fear.

"SNAP OUT OF IT!" he yells.

It doesn't work. Anger thinks fast. If he wants to help Fear, he'll probably have to act more like Joy.

"Hey, Fear!" he says, trying to talk in a high, peppy voice. "It's me, Joy! You're back in Headquarters. Isn't it super?"

Fear blinks. "Joy?" he asks. Then he focuses. "Hey, this isn't Headquarters."

Before Fear can freeze again, Anger grabs his arm. "Come on! Let's get out of here!"

He turns toward the door—and Jangles is there!

"The party's not over yet," says Jangles.

"Time for the bouncy pit!"

Jangles reaches out with his white gloves and picks up Fear and Anger. He tosses them into a pit of colorful plastic balls.

"What the—" Anger yells. He tries to get to his feet but tumbles around in the balls.

Fear freak outs again. "Remember when Riley sank into the ball pit and couldn't get out? Mom had to come in and rescue her. It was awful!"

Then they hear a *honk!* followed by the sound of floppy feet stomping toward them.

"Jangles wants to play!"

"Quick! Hide!" Fear cries, ducking under some balls.

"I'm getting tired of this big bozo," Anger says. "I say we get out of here!"

If they hide, go to page 123.

If Anger tries to get them out of the ball pit, go to page 109.

"I'm telling you, it's this green memory!" Disgust says, grabbing it. Then she runs off to throw it in the Memory Dump.

"STOP!" Anger yells. "You can look into the sphere to see if it's the right memory!"

"Really?" Disgust asks. She skids to a stop— and then trips. The sphere falls out of her hand and tumbles into the Memory Dump below!

"How do we know if that was the right dream?" Rainbow Unicorn asks.

"We have to go back and look at the purple memory," Anger replies. "Come on!"

Just then, the Forgetters arrive.

Rainbow Unicorn takes off. "I'm out of here! You two are on your own."

"You're under arrest for messing with our memories," says one Forgetter.

Disgust and Anger look at each other.

"Run!" they both yell.

They dash past the Forgetters and come

to a long spiral staircase and head down. The stairs lead to a massive gate.

Disgust looks behind her and sees that the Forgetters are at the top of the stairs, too afraid to go down.

"Maybe we shouldn't go through here," she says, but Anger is way ahead of her.

"Stop right there!" Two guards stand at the gate. They grab Anger and Disgust.

"Send them to the Subconscious," says one guard.

"Oh no! Sadness told us about the Subconscious. It's creepy in there. Please don't do this," Disgust begs.

But the guards don't listen. They shove Disgust and Anger through the door of a spooky-looking cave and slam the door shut.

"Noooo!" Disgust cries. The cave is filled with the sounds of thunder, circus music, and roaring dinosaurs. She turns around so she can pound on the door—but it's blocked by a huge stalk of broccoli.

Anger cracks his knuckles. "No problem. I'll just push it aside." He gives the giant stalk a shove. It doesn't budge.

"I could use a little help here," he says.

"Are you serious?" Disgust asks. "That's broccoli. BROCCOLI! These hands will never touch broccoli!"

If Disgust helps Anger move the broccoli stalk, go to page 55.

If they explore a creepy tunnel instead, go to page 51.

**(continued from page 110)**

Anger carries Fear to Goofball Island. It's the part of Riley's personality that helps her to be silly and have fun.

When they arrive, happy carnival music fills the air. Anger puts Fear in front of a colorful merry-go-round. The animals on the ride look bright and happy. There are a big pink elephant, a yellow bunny, a purple cow, and more.

Fear starts to smile.

"All better?" Anger asks.

"This is nice," says Fear, sitting down on a bench. "Let's stay here for a while."

"Sorry, but we've got to go," says Anger. "We still have to stop that jingle. And then we need to get back to Headquarters before Riley wakes up."

"No way," says Fear. "I'm not going back out there. This is nice. I could get used to it here."

"Come on," Anger says. "Riley needs us."

Fear thinks for a minute. Then he looks

behind him, out at the islands, the Memory Dump, and the shelves of Long Term Memory.

"Nope," he says finally. "No telling what else we'll find out there. I'm staying put."

Anger tries to pick him up.    "If you won't go, I'll carry you!"

"Hey," Fear protests, slapping him away. "Get off me!"

Anger sighs. He doesn't want to do this by force. Then he spots something past the merry-go-round.

It's a carnival game where you shoot a water gun into the center of a plastic flower. The flower rises up a pole and dings a bell at the top. The first player to ring the bell wins.

Anger looks at Fear. "Tell you what. Let's play the game. If I win, you come back to Headquarters with me. If you win, you can stay here."

Fear thinks about this and decides it's worth a try. Otherwise, Anger will probably drag him out of there kicking and screaming.

"Okay," he says.

If Fear wins the game, go to page 66.

If Anger wins, go to page 71.

(continued from page 99)

Fear tries to remember what Joy and Sadness told him about the train station. Was it something about a shortcut?

He looks around and sees a walled-in place with gates not too far from the Long Term Memory shelves. Maybe the shortcut is through there. Fear jogs toward it.

He can hear happy music behind the walls. He steps inside.

There's a forest of giant French fries in front of him.

"Giant French fries can only mean one thing," he says. "A giant, hungry monster who loves fast food!"

Fear's heart begins to pound. In a panic, he runs away from the giant fries.

Suddenly, he feels the ground wobble beneath him. Curious, he stops and looks around.

He seems to be in Riley's old living room back

in Minnesota. He's standing on a green ottoman. Instead of the nice brown carpet beneath him, the floor is a pool of bubbling hot lava.

"Heeeeeeeeeeeelp!" Fear screams.

Anger appears at the edge of the lava pool, out of breath.

"Oh, great!" he says. "How did you get there? This is that game that Riley used to play when she was little, remember? She'd pretend the floor was made of lava and jump from one piece of furniture to another without falling into it. But this is Imagination Land. Here, it's real!"

"Just get me out!" Fear yells.

If Anger plays the lava game to save Fear, go to page 91.

If Anger tries another way to save Fear, go to page 103.

(continued from page 74)

Anger glances back at Disgust. She's smoothing her hair and making model poses.

"Forget it! She can catch up to me," he says, and walks out of Trophy Town. "I'm on some dumb search for French fries and all she can do is look at her face! I never should have brought her. I should have— What?"

Anger has been too upset to notice that he's walked right into Cloud Town. Fluffy white clouds surround him. He's stepped right on top of one.

The cloud slowly floats into the air with Anger on it.

"Hey! Quit it!" he yells at the cloud. "STOP RIGHT NOW!"

*Whoosh!* The sheer force of his yell sends the cloud shooting out of Imagination Land. It floats over to Long Term Memory and stops. Anger tumbles off the cloud and lands on a memory shelf, in front of a recall tube.

"Fine! I give up!" he cries. He climbs into the recall tube and gets sucked into Headquarters.

"You're back!" Fear cries, hugging him. "Did you get rid of the jingle?"

"No!" Anger fumes.

"Hey, where's Disgust?" Joy asks.

"Staring at her reflection in the trophies in Trophy Town," he reports. "I couldn't get her to leave."

"I knew it," says Sadness. "We'll never see her again."

"We will, too," Joy tells her, "because you are going back there to get her. You'll have to wait until tomorrow night, though. Riley's going to wake up soon."

"I sure hope you can bring her back," Sadness says.

## THE END

"Let's find that spider memory," Anger says. "It's in Long Term Memory. We can look for the Forgetters there, too."

Disgust frowns. "But that will take too long. We've got to get this done before Riley wakes up."

"I'll help you," Rainbow Unicorn offers. "Anything to be the star of Riley's dreams again!"

Rainbow Unicorn takes one of the gold carts that the Dream Productions crew uses to get around the studio. Anger and Disgust climb in. They quickly zip to the shelves of Long Term Memory. The shelves are mostly gleaming with happy, golden memories. But there are a few red, blue, green, and purple ones mixed in, too.

"There are millions of memories here! How are we supposed to find the spider one?" Disgust asks as they climb off the cart.

"Joy has been having me read mind manuals to calm my nerves," Anger says. "I think I can figure it out. Do you remember when the spider memory happened?"

"Of course I do," Disgust says. "It was the day after Halloween a few years ago. Riley tripped over a log and found a spider nest." She shudders.

"Hmm. Halloween. What costume was Riley wearing?" Anger asks.

"A pink princess dress," Disgust says.

"I know exactly when that was! Mom ordered a YELLOW princess dress, but the PINK one came instead. Boy, was I mad!"

Anger stomps down the aisle, followed by Disgust and Rainbow Unicorn. He follows twists and turns and finally comes to a stop in front of one of the shelves.

"Here we go. Halloween three years

ago should be somewhere around here," he says.

"Look! There's a green memory. That must be the memory of the spiders," Disgust says. "I was sooo grossed out when I saw them."

"There's a purple one right near it," says Anger. "Do you remember how much Riley screamed when she saw those spiders? That's got to be a Fear memory."

"Will you two just hurry up and pick one already?" says Rainbow Unicorn. "The spotlight is waiting for me."

If Disgust and Anger choose the purple memory sphere, go to page 20.

If they choose the green memory sphere, go to page 78.

Anger surveys the living room setup. Fear's ottoman is floating near the coffee table. To get to the coffee table, he'll have to jump onto the couch.

Anger takes a few steps back so he can take a running leap.

"Are you crazy?" Fear yells. "Those stubby little legs of yours will never make it to the couch!"

"Do you want me to save you or not?" Anger asks, and Fear bites his lip.

"All right. Here we go . . . ," Anger says. He runs as fast as he can until he reaches the edge of the lava. Then he takes a leap.

*Whomp!* He lands on the couch and tumbles over. But he doesn't fall off.

"Told you!" says Anger. From there it's an easy jump to the coffee table. Then he jumps onto the ottoman. It rocks underneath his feet, and Fear almost slides off.

"Hey!" Fear yells as Anger grabs him.

"Gotcha!" Anger says. "Now let's do this."

Holding Fear, Anger jumps back to the coffee table, then back to the couch. Then he makes a mighty leap to shore.

"Ow! Ow! Ow!" Anger yells as the back of his feet splash down in the lava.

Fear hops out of his arms. "You okay, buddy?"

"I am NOT okay," Anger says. "And I'm going to tell you exactly what's going to happen. You are going back to Headquarters and I am staying here. Got it?"

Fear doesn't argue. "Got it," he says.

## THE END

"Give me a push and I'll try to grab the fork," Disgust says.

Anger is stubborn. "I'm telling you, I can reach that fry."

Anger strains and stretches his stubby arms as far as he can. He pulls down the soggy French fry and grabs hold.

"Come on!" he yells.

Grimacing, Disgust wades through the thick ketchup and grabs onto the fry. Anger pulls himself along the fry, splashing ketchup as he moves.

"Hey! Watch it!" Disgust complains.

Anger gets to the edge of the ketchup just as the French fry breaks and sends Disgust tumbling into the ketchup. He quickly reaches out and pulls her up, but she's covered from head to toe.

"Need. Shower. Now," she says.

"Let's get this fry back to the Forgetters

and get out of here," Anger says.

They head back to Long Term Memory, but the Forgetters aren't happy with the soggy, ketchup-covered fry.

"Seeing one up close isn't as exciting as I thought it would be," one Forgetter says with a frown.

"Hey," says Anger. "We brought you a French fry, just like you asked. A deal's a deal."

The Forgetters whisper to each other and then break apart.

"Okay," one says. "We'll get rid of the Minyblast jingle."

"Can we *please* go back to Headquarters now?" Disgust begs.

The Forgetters lead them to a recall tube and they get whisked back to Headquarters.

"Aaaah! They're covered in blood!" Fear yells when he sees them.

"It's ketchup," says Disgust. "I'm getting it

off me right now."

"Glad you guys made it," Joy says. "Riley will be awake soon."

A short while later, Anger and Disgust are clean and Riley is waking up. As she does, a new memory rolls in from the recall tube.

"Uh-oh," says Sadness.

Riley walks to the bathroom and picks up a tube of toothpaste.

*"Denta-Clean, for the cleanest teeth!"* she sings.

"Looks like Riley's got a new jingle in her head," Sadness says.

Anger smacks his fist into his hand. "Those Forgetters! They tricked me!"

# THE END

(continued from page 15)

"This is a one-man job," Anger insists. "She can go tomorrow night."

"If you don't bring someone with you, something terrible will probably happen and you'll never come back," says Sadness. "We'd really miss you."

Fear gasps. "Something terrible? Don't do this, buddy. You don't have to go at all. We can live with the jingle!"

"Maybe *you* can live with it, but I can't," Anger says. He jumps into the memory tube. "So long!"

*Whoosh!* The tube sucks him in. Fear panics.

"No! You can't go alone! Something terrible will happen!" he yells.

Fear jumps into the tube after Anger!

Joy, Disgust, and Sadness look at one another.

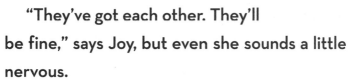

Sadness shakes her head. "He won't last very long out there," she says.

"They've got each other. They'll be fine," says Joy, but even she sounds a little nervous.

Inside the tube, Fear is screaming his head off.

"Aaaaaah!" he shrieks. "Toooooo faaaaaast!"

*Thump!* The tube spits out Anger and he lands on the ground. But skinny Fear shoots out of the tube like a kid on a waterslide. He soars through the air. . . .

*Thump!* He finally lands. He lifts up his head— and sees that he's right on the edge of a cliff!

"Aaaaaaaaaaaaaah!" he screams. Down below is a dizzying drop filled with discarded memory spheres. It's the Memory Dump that Joy and Sadness told him about.

Fear jumps up and looks around. Over by the tube, Anger is calling him, but his heart is pounding so loud he can barely hear his own name.

It's all so . . . big. Headquarters is nice and cozy and safe. Here, things go on and on in every direction. Behind him, Fear can see rows and rows of long shelves. Beyond the

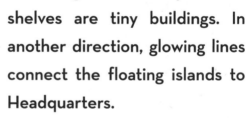

shelves are tiny buildings. In another direction, glowing lines connect the floating islands to Headquarters.

"I never should have come here!" Fear cries. All he can think about is getting out. But how?

He remembers Joy and Sadness saying something about a recall tube, but he can't remember where it's supposed to be.

There has to be some other way out, right?

He looks around. Maybe there's an elevator in those buildings. Then he remembers Joy and Sadness talking about a Train of Thought that goes right to Headquarters.

If Fear runs toward the buildings, go to page 24.

If Fear tries to find the train station, go to page 84.

(continued from page 74)

Anger sighs. He can't leave Disgust behind. But how will he get her away from her reflection? Suddenly, he has an idea.

Like a bull, Anger charges at the trophy Disgust is looking at. He rams into it headfirst.

"Hey!" Disgust yells, jumping back.

*Bam!*

The trophy topples and knocks over the one beside it. Then that trophy topples over, and they all begin to fall like dominoes.

"Why did you do that?" Disgust asks.

"To get you out of here," Anger says, grabbing her hand. "Come on!"

They run through Trophy Town and come out in front of what looks like a village of clouds.

"Is nothing easy here?" Anger wonders.

Anger and Disgust dodge

through Cloud Town, weaving their way around the fluffy, floating clouds, but it's impossible to avoid them. They bump right into a fat cloud. It picks them up and carries them off.

"Stop this right now!" Anger yells at the cloud.

The cloud can't go far with two Emotions on it, so it settles down on the nearest island. Pop music is blaring.

"Ooh, I love this song," squeals Disgust, jumping off the cloud.

"Ohhhhh no. No you don't!" cries Anger, trying to stop her. But Disgust races off toward the sound of the music.

When Anger catches up to her, Disgust is standing in front of a screen showing five boys singing onstage. Pop music blares from speakers nearby.

"Woo-hoo!" cheers Disgust, jumping up

and down as she stares at the screen. "I love you!"

*This is Boy Band Island,* Anger realizes. "I'll never get her out of here!"

If Anger decides to leave Disgust once and for all, go to page 34.

If Anger comes up with a plan to get Disgust away from Boy Band Island, go to page 126.

*(continued from page 85)*

Anger tries to remember what Joy and Sadness told him about Imagination Land. Then he gets an idea.

"Be right back," he tells Fear.

Moments later, he comes floating by on a cloud from Cloud Town. Fear's eyes grow wide.

"Is that thing safe?" he asks.

"Safer than lava," Anger says. He holds out his hand. "Climb on!"

Fear looks up at the cloud, then down at the lava. He wrings his hands. It's a tough choice.

With a sigh, Anger pulls him onto the cloud.

"Hey!" Fear cries. "Where are we going, anyway?"

"Wherever this cloud takes us, I guess," Anger says, as the wind pushes them out of Imagination Land.

# THE END

(continued from page 61)

Disgust nudges him. "Apologize! They're not going to help if you don't."

"They're the ones who should be apologizing to *me*, for sending that rotten jingle back up to Headquarters!" yells Anger. He faces the two Forgetters. "I will *not* apologize. Now get rid of that jingle or else!"

One of the Forgetters eyes him. "Or else what?"

"Or else . . . you'll be sorry!" says Anger.

"Well, our 'or else' is worse than your 'or else,'" says the other Forgetter.

"What does that mean?" asks Anger.

The Forgetter points a vacuum at him.

*Whoosh!* Anger gets sucked into the vacuum. He shoots through a tube, twisting and turning, and then he shoots out.

Dazed, Anger looks around. He expects to be in the Memory Dump, but this looks like one of Riley's Islands of Personality. He's in the middle of the woods. Tall pine trees tower over him.

"Which one of Riley's islands is this?" he wonders out loud.

Then he sees a screen up ahead. On it, a girl is wandering through the forest with a dreamy look in her eyes.

"I'm looking for vampires," she says.

"Looking for vampires?" asks Anger. "Shouldn't she be running away from them?"

"I think vampires are soooo cute," the girl says. "My boyfriend is a vampire!"

Suddenly, Anger realizes where they are. "Oh no," he says. This is Tragic Vampire Romance Island! He's never understood why Riley liked those goofy books. Vampires are supposed to be scary, not romantic. This is the worst place he could have ended up!

"Curse you, Forgetters!" he yells.

## THE END

*(continued from page 23)*

Anger and Disgust race toward Honesty Island. Once they're on the island, they see the Forgetters scurrying toward them.

"I knew we should have looked for those Forgetters first," Anger fumes. "I wish you'd never . . . I mean . . . um . . ."

"Just say it," Disgust demands. "You wish I had never come with you."

"That's what I wanted to say, but I couldn't get the words out," Anger admits. "Darned Honesty Island! You can't tell anything but the truth here. And the truth is, . . . I don't mind that you came. You're not so bad."

"Oh yeah?" says Disgust. "Well, I think you're . . . not so bad, too."

Anger and Disgust smile at each other—and then the Forgetters reach them.

"Hands up! You're going to the Memory Dump!" one yells.

The other Forgetter turns to him. "Do you know your voice sounds like a dying moose?"

"Really? Well, your voice sounds like a sick goose!" says the other.

Anger and Disgust look at each other. Honesty Island is making the Forgetters be honest with each other.

"Your jokes aren't funny!"

"You walk pigeon-toed!"

Seeing their chance, Anger and Disgust slip away.

"Where to now?" Disgust asks.

"Let's get back to Headquarters," Anger says. "If the Forgetters ever get off that island, I have a feeling they won't want to take any of my suggestions."

They go back to Long Term Memory and

find a recall tube in the shelves, just as Joy and Sadness had told them they would.

*Whoosh!* They get sucked back into Headquarters. Fear tackles them with a relieved hug.

"You made it!" he cries.

"Hands off!" Anger says. "Yes, we're back. We got rid of the spider dream. But I guess we're going to have to live with the jingle."

Sadness sighs. "That's too bad. I guess poor Riley will never get it out of her head."

"Well, I'm just happy we're all together again," says Joy. "And look! A new dream!"

On the screen, Rainbow Unicorn is tap-dancing.

"Is that the best she could come up with?" Disgust asks. "Lame!"

# THE END

(continued from page 77)

Anger doesn't want to hide. He starts crushing the balls in the ball pit one by one.

*Pop! Pop! Pop!* Fear puts his hands over his ears—and so does Jangles.

"This isn't a fun party!" says Jangles. He stomps off with his big feet.

Anger pulls Fear out of the ball pit. He's so scared that he's frozen like a Popsicle. Anger picks him up and marches out of the Subconscious.

"Stop right there!" yell the guards.

"See my friend here?" asks Anger. "Jangles did this to him. Let us go, or I'll tell him you two want to play."

The guards turn pale and quickly open the gates. Anger marches up the stairs with Fear but then stops. He's got to figure out what to do next.

He could take Fear back to Headquarters and hope he returns to normal. But he knows the other Emotions will blame him for not keeping Fear safe. There's got to be some other way to snap Fear out of it.

"Puppy dogs," Fear mutters. "Lollipops. Soft, fluffy pillows."

"That's it!" Anger says. He needs to get Fear to a friendly place filled with happy things. Then maybe he'll thaw out.

If Anger takes Fear to Goofball Island, go to page 81.

If he takes him to Friendship Island, go to page 49.

"Let's go to the right," Disgust says. "Right is my lucky direction."

"Who even has a lucky direction?" Anger asks.

"I do," Disgust says. "Come on, let's go."

They walk across the plateau toward Imagination Land. When they get close, they can see lots of crazy colors inside. But it's hard to tell what's going on behind the gates.

When they enter through the gate on the right, they find themselves in a forest of giant French fries. The fries tower over them like trees.

"We're in luck!" says Anger.

"I told you right was lucky," says Disgust.

They spot a giant plastic fork on the ground and use it to chop down two perfect fries. Then they bring them back to the Forgetters.

"Gee, that was fast," says one Forgetter.

"That *was* fast," says the other.

"You're welcome," says Anger. "Now it's time to keep your end of the bargain. Get rid of that gum jingle!"

The two Forgetters whisper to each other and then look back at Anger.

"That was too easy," one Forgetter says.

"Way too easy," the other agrees. "We want you to do something else for us."

Smoke comes out of Anger's ears. "Something else? Are you serious? Something else? WE HAD A DEAL!"

"Um, he's got a point," says Disgust. "We did have a deal."

The Forgetters look smug.

"We make the rules around here," says the boy Forgetter. "So what's it going to be? Will you do something else for us or not?"

Anger looks as if he's about to explode. "WE ABSOLUTELY WILL N—"

Disgust interrupts him. "Cool down. Let's talk about this first."

If Anger and Disgust agree to the new request, go to page 27.

If they say forget it, go to page 52.

(continued from page 50)

Anger and Fear make the trip back to Long Term Memory. There, they find two blue creatures. Anger knows right away that they're Forgetters. "You!" he says. "I have a problem with you two!"

The Forgetters frown.

"Oh yeah?" asks one Forgetter.

"Yeah," says Anger. "You need to get that Mintyblast jingle out of Riley's mind. It's driving her crazy!"

The Forgetters giggle.

"Oh, come on," says the other Forgetter. "It's fun!"

"Fun? Are you kidding?" says Fear. "That jingle is dangerous!"

"What do you mean?" asks the first Forgetter.

"What if she's humming the jingle and gets distracted while crossing the street?" Fear asks.

"Well—" The Forgetter starts to protest, but

Fear interrupts him before he can finish.

"What if she hums it in class and gets in trouble?" he asks. "What if she can't remember her spelling words because the jingle gets in the way? What if she's humming it during a hockey game and doesn't see the puck flying toward her and gets hit? What if—"

"Okay, okay!" says the other Forgetter. "We'll get rid of it."

"You will?" asks Anger.

"Promise," he replies.

Anger looks at Fear and smiles. He hates to admit it, but it's a good thing Fear came along.

## THE END

"Ha!" says Anger. "I win! Let's go find those Forgetters!"

"Fine," Disgust grumbles, crossing her arms in front of her. "So how will we find them, anyway?"

"Sadness says they hang out in the Long Term Memory shelves, looking for old memories that Riley no longer needs so they can vacuum them up and send them to the Memory Dump," Anger tells her.

"Mind workers with vacuums. Right," says Disgust. "So how did these janitors get so much power over Riley's memory?"

Anger shrugs. "I don't know, but it sure is annoying," he says. "And what's even more annoying is that they have the power to send any memory they want back up through the recall tubes. Like that jingle . . ." Steam starts to rise from his flat red head.

"Okay, I get it, you want to get rid of the

jingle," Disgust says. "Let's hurry up and find those vacuumers so we can get rid of the spider dream next."

The Emotions start walking through the twisting, turning shelves that hold Riley's memories. It's not long before they see two small blue creatures scurrying among the shelves. Each of them is holding a vacuum.

"Forgetters!" Anger yells, quickly stomping toward them. "I've got a beef with you!"

One of the Forgetters giggles and pokes Anger in the stomach. "Looks like you've had a lot of beef!"

Anger scowls. "You're a funny guy, huh? Well, I'll tell you what's not funny. That stupid Mintyblast jingle. Get rid of it!"

"And who are you to tell us what to do, beef-a-rooney?" asks the other Forgetter.

"Yeah, who are you, anyway?" her partner asks.

Anger clenches his fists. "I'll tell you who I am—"

"Maybe you should let me handle this," Disgust whispers in his ear. "The way you're going about it, they'll never do us a favor."

If Anger lets Disgust handle the situation, go to page 16.

If Anger continues to handle it himself, go to page 61.

"This way!" Anger yells. They race to Hockey Island.

The island is filled with awesome hockey stuff—a rink, giant hockey sticks, a big trophy, and a huge scoreboard. Disgust and Anger run into a nearby equipment shed to hide.

"Is this your plan?" Disgust asks. "This is the first place they'll come looking."

"Why am I supposed to be the one with the plan?" Anger asks.

"Because you're the one who said we should hide here!" Disgust shoots back.

Then they hear the Forgetters outside.

"They're in there! I heard them!" says one.

Disgust turns to Anger. "I told you."

Anger grabs a hockey stick off the wall and picks up a puck with his other hand.

"Don't worry," he says, his eyes narrowing. "I got this."

The two Forgetters burst into the shed, holding their vacuums.

"Hold it right there, you two!" one Forgetter says.

"I don't know how to play nice," says Anger. He drops the puck and whacks it with the hockey stick.

*Bam!* The puck hits one of the vacuums and sends it flying out of the Forgetter's hands.

"Hey!" the Forgetter protests.

Anger picks up another puck.

*Bam!* The other vacuum goes flying.

"Hey!" protests the other Forgetter.

Anger picks up a third puck. "Who's next?" he asks with a gleam in his eyes.

The Forgetters turn and run out of the shed.

"Well, that worked," says Disgust. "Now let's get back to Headquarters."

Anger runs out of the equipment shed, still

holding the puck. "Are you kidding? This is too much fun!"

He hops into the ice rink and starts batting the puck around.

"Woo-hoo!" he cheers as Disgust rolls her eyes.

Back in Headquarters, the other Emotions are worried.

"The spider dream is gone, but where are Anger and Disgust?" Fear asks.

"Trapped forever, probably," says Sadness. "I'll really miss them."

"They'll be back," says Joy hopefully. "I just hope they return before Riley wakes up."

# THE END

(continued from page 77)

Fear pulls Anger down with him and they hide under the balls. Above them, they hear the footsteps stop.

"Where's the party?" Jangles asks sadly. Fear is holding his breath, afraid to make a sound. To his relief, he hears Jangles yawn.

"Sleepy now," says Jangles, and then the floppy shoes stomp off.

Fear and Anger climb out of the ball pit.

They find themselves in a dark hallway. They follow it back to the Subconscious entrance and push open the door.

"Stop right there!" one of the guards shouts.

"I'd lower my voice if I were you," says Fear. "Jangles just went down for a nap."

At the sound of Jangles's name, the guards turn pale.

"So we'll be leaving now," says Anger. "Unless you want me to get loud. Because I can get really loud!"

"No, no, no, that's fine," say the guards. They quickly open the gates for Anger and Fear. The two Emotions run up the stairs.

"Let's go find those Forgetters and get rid of that jingle," says Anger.

Fear nods toward a nearby building. "Let's go to Dream Productions and get rid of that spider dream. I'm pretty sick of that thing."

"But we don't have t—" Anger begins. It's no use. Fear is already jogging ahead of him.

Anger catches up to Fear at the entrance to Dream Productions. Fear takes a deep breath and then he opens the door.

"Aaaaaaaaaaaaaaaaaah!"

Actors wearing spider costumes are wiggling their fake legs on a movie set. A computer monitor shows what Riley sees in her dream—super-creepy spiders.

Fear starts running back and forth.

"Spiders! Help!" he shrieks.

He knocks over boxes of props. Pool noodles spill onto the set and turn into snakes. Ping-Pong balls turn into bouncing eyeballs.

In Headquarters, Disgust sees the new dream on the screen. "If this dream gets any creepier, Riley might wake up."

Back in Dream Productions, the director stomps up to Anger, holding a kitten costume.

"Put this on and get in there!" she demands, shoving the costume into his hands. "And calm him down," she says, pointing to Fear.

If Anger wears the kitten costume, go to page 58.

If Anger refuses to wear the costume, go to page 32.

**(continued from page 102)**

"This is the last time I'm going to help her," Anger mutters. He scans the scene and sees just what he needs: an electric guitar in a stand on the side of the screen.

He picks up the guitar, straps it across his chest, raises his right hand, and . . .

*Vrooom!* He plays the loudest, angriest chord ever heard on Boy Band Island. Anger strums the strings again, and a screeching heavy metal sound rips across the stage.

Disgust puts her hands over her ears.

"Stop!" she yells. "It sounds like a train full of angry cats!"

Victorious, Anger jumps offstage and walks up to her.

"Show's over," he says. "Let's get out of here."

Anger and Disgust walk back to Imagination Land. This time, they enter through the gate on the right. In front of them is French Fry Forest.

Tall golden French fries tower over them like trees.

"Great," says Anger. "Of course these couldn't be normal, everyday French fries. Let's find a skinny one and try to knock it down."

Disgust frowns. "But they're so greasy."

"I'm not doing this by myself," Anger insists. "Come on!"

Disgust follows Anger into French Fry Forest. Suddenly, she feels something squishy under her feet. She looks down. Red stuff is oozing over her shoes.

"Gross!" she yells. Then she realizes that she's sinking.

Anger is a few steps ahead of her. He's stuck in the sticky red stuff, too. He dips a finger into it and sniffs.

"Ketchup!" he cries. "We're stuck in a condiment!"

"Oh, that's just great," says Disgust, spotting

a giant plastic fork on the shores of the quick-sand. "I'm not touching that greasy thing. We should try to reach that fork."

If Disgust and Anger reach for the fork, go to page 41.

If they reach for the French fry, go to page 93.

128